M000169826

Contents

Bea Mine

WITH BONUS STORY, BLESS YOUR HEART

KRISTEN DIXON

THIGPEN-
GANDY
PUBLISHING

THIGPEN-GANDY PUBLISHING

ONE

Love makes you stupid. There, I said it. There's no plausible excuse that can explain my predicament otherwise. What predicament? Oh, the one where I was standing there frozen like a statue—with a batch of muffins—inside George Anderson's apartment, unbeknownst to him. Did I mention that I could hear him in the entryway, chatting with a giggling woman? No? Let me back up to the beginning.

One week earlier

It was Wednesday afternoon at the bakery, and I was making cupcakes and taking specialty orders for Valentine's Day. Sweet Mr. Harris had placed his order for a half dozen heart-shaped cookies for his pregnant wife, Leanne, when the door chime sounded, again. It had been chiming non-stop all day, which meant I'd had no lunch break yet and it was already two p.m. With a sigh, I glanced up from ringing in his order to see who the next customer was, and felt my smile freeze on my face. Like clockwork, George was here for his Wednesday afternoon snack. *George Anderson, you handsome devil.*

I managed a quick nod of acknowledgement in his direction and tried to focus back in on Mr. Harris's cookie order.

"That'll be fifteen dollars," I said before taking his debit card. "Would you like delivery, or pickup?" *George Anderson, you can pick me up any time you want.*

"Is there an extra charge for delivery? I'd love to surprise her at work."

"No sir, Valentine's Day special. All deliveries are free the thirteenth through fifteenth." I gave him a polite smile, but George's looming presence behind him stole my attention.

"Oh, that's wonderful! Then yes, I'd like delivery," Mr. Harris said with a smile.

"Great, if you'd just fill out this delivery slip for me, you'll be all set up," I said, passing him the pink paper.

As Mr. Harris wrote in Leanne's work address and his desired delivery time, I tried my hardest not to stare past him at George, who was standing patiently with his hands in his pockets, perusing the chalkboard menu behind my head. The seconds ticked by slower than molasses, but Mr. Harris finally handed the delivery sheet back over, and I tucked it into the overflowing file with the rest of the town's orders. We were still five days out from Valentine's Day, and already it was shaping up to be our busiest yet.

"Have a nice day, Mr. Harris," I said with forced cheer as he left. No longer able to hide behind a smitten husband, I turned my full attention on George. Medium height with a lean-muscled build and tousled blonde hair—his gorgeous smile was enough to make my knees knock. But I certainly wasn't going to tell him that.

"Hi, George. What can I get for you today?" I said, voice carefully neutral. *Candlelight dinner, table for two?*

"Well, everything looks delicious," he said, and his gaze seemed to linger on my lips.

You're imagining things again, Bea. He's known you since you were seven, he's had plenty of chances and he's not interested.

"But I think I'll have to go with a blueberry muffin to go, and a small coffee, black." He rocked back on his heels, hands still in his jeans pockets.

"Okay, I'll be happy to get that for you. Let me run in the back and get you a muffin—all we have up here are the strawberry cheesecake special."

Note to self: find out if they make a blueberry muffin lip gloss.

"Take your time, I'm in no hurry," he said, giving me another stunning smile.

Regardless, I hurried. The quicker he's gone, the quicker I can get my head back to reality, and out of daydreams of George whisking me away to a tropical honeymoon. I pushed open the swinging double doors to the small kitchen, and in my haste nearly ran smack into Celia, the owner.

"Great Moses, where's the fire?" Celia asked, catching me by the shoulders right before we collided.

"Goodness, sorry Celia. There's no fire, I need a fresh blueberry muffin for an order," I said, embarrassed.

"Well, we've got a hot dozen right on the back counter." She gestured to the jumbo-sized muffins still cooling in the tin.

I bustled over and tried to grab one, but they were so hot I scorched the side of my hand on the tin. "Shoot!" I shook my hand to ease the burning sensation.

Celia took me in while she dried her hands on a pink towel, a look of curiosity on her face. "You okay, darlin'? It's not like you to be clumsy, and you've nearly taken out both of us in ninety seconds flat."

I crossed to the sink and stuck my burnt hand under cold running water to take out the sting. I shook my head, my expression sheepish. "I'm fine, Celia. Just being an airhead this afternoon—you know how it is sometimes."

She cocked one eyebrow and set the towel down. "I see. Well, you let that hand cool off for a bit, and I'll take the muffin out." She grabbed a slip of parchment paper and deftly lifted the sugar-topped muffin without touching the pan and breezed out the swinging doors to deliver it to George.

The sound of light chatter reached me, and after another minute of soaking, my hand felt better, so I turned off the faucet and carefully dried it on Celia's abandoned towel. I walked over to the swinging doors but instead of heading back out, I hovered just inside, listening for a moment.

"Well, George, I'm really in a tight spot this week. You see, Julian, my usual delivery driver, has the flu, and won't be able to do any deliveries for at least a week. And Valentine's Day is our busiest delivery day of the entire *year*, as I'm sure you can imagine." Celia paused.

"Well now, that is a predicament. You don't have a backup driver?" George asked.

"No, we're a small business, and the rest of the year we don't have the order volume to keep another driver busy. I know I could hire a temporary person, but I hate to trust someone I don't know with our most important sales day of the year. We have a pristine reputation to maintain, after all."

I stifled a snort. *As if there is anybody in this whole county Celia doesn't know personally! What is she getting at?*

"You're right, a temporary person isn't ideal. What are you going to do?"

"Well, I was hoping I'd be able to find a strapping young lad to help out for the day. You wouldn't happen to be available, would you? Handsome as you are, I'm sure you already have plans with a lady friend," Celia said with an innocent tone.

6

in Tennessee when a knock at the front door interrupted my Danish shaping. After settling the current heart-shaped pastry onto the baking sheet with its neighbors, I pushed through the swinging doors to see who was here an hour before opening time.

There, on the other side of the glass door with a heart-stopping smile and a wave, was George. Knees suddenly wobbly, I tried to keep a casual air as I unlocked the door to let him in.

"Hey George, what are you doing here? We don't open for another hour . . ."

He grabbed his chest with exaggeration, "Why Bea, you act like you aren't happy to see me, your newest co-worker! And here I thought you and I were friends," he said with a wink.

Friend-zoned, as always. The gloomy thought tried to strangle me, but I pushed it aside and forced a smile as I walked back to the counter. "You know we are, George. Daphne wouldn't have it any other way."

He grinned. "Exactly. Now, I have a *serious* question for you."

I froze behind the counter, heart pounding. "Oh yeah, what's that?" *Act casual, act casual!*

"Are employees entitled to early muffins and coffee? Because I could really use some of that sweetness for the day I have ahead of me." He waggled his eyebrows, completely unaware of the mental rollercoaster his words caused me.

"Ahh, sure, George. I can grab you a muffin. I haven't started the coffee yet, though. So, it will be a few minutes for that." I kept my disappointment locked firmly inside and leaned on my professionalism.

"That's no problem, I'm not in a hurry. Can I help you with anything in the meantime? I know you have a lot to get done before the shop opens, right?" He gestured towards the kitchen in the back.

"Do you know how to bake?" I asked, surprised by the offer.

"Not a lick, but I bet you're an excellent teacher. Come on, put me to work. Celia already did." His smile is so genuine, I can never turn it down. It pierces straight to my heart every time.

"All right, I'm sure I can find something for you to do. Come on." I walk back to the kitchen, and he follows me.

Scanning the room for a job to give him, my eyes landed on the sugar cookie dough already rolled and waiting to be cut out.

"How do you feel about sugar cookies?" I asked, turning to face him. He was wearing a sky-blue but-

I rummaged in the fridge for the creamer and poured it into the white ceramic pitcher. I then grabbed a still-warm blueberry muffin—without burning myself this time—and followed him to the front of the shop.

He was spooning a large heap of sugar into his coffee when the doors swung shut with a bang—my hands too full to stop it. He jolted in surprise, and sugar scattered over the coffee bar. "Shoot!" he mumbled and tried to wipe it up with his hand.

I walked over and set the cream pitcher down, then put a hand on his forearm. "Leave it, I'll get a rag."

His eyes locked on my hand where it connected with his skin, before traveling to meet my eyes. Wordlessly, he nodded. It took my brain a moment to get my feet to move away from him. One tiny, innocent touch and I was rooted to the spot. I hurried to grab a rag, and wiped up the sugar mess. He hovered to the side holding his coffee and muffin, looking pensive.

As soon as I finished, he spoke. "Thanks for letting me crash your prep time this morning."

"Oh, no big deal. You are my newest co-worker, after all," I tried to joke, but it felt flat.

His lips turned up in a half smile. "That's right. Well, I'd better go and let you get back at it. I left some cash on the counter to cover this." He jiggled his muffin, which was already missing a bite.

"Okay, thanks for helping with the cookies. Sorry about your pants." I gestured awkwardly in the direction of his leg.

He chuckled, "Any time. See you later, Bea." He turned and walked out of the door, the small chime echoing in the bakery—the space suddenly empty without him in it.

Deflated, I sagged against the countertop with a sigh. My emotions were all over the place this week. One thing was for sure—something was up with George Anderson. Only, I couldn't figure out *what*.

THREE

The workday thankfully passed in a distracted blur. I was a little slow getting all the morning prep done, but I caught up in the mid-morning lull after the early work rush. Celia gave me a few side-long glances throughout the day, seeming to pick up on my preoccupation. Thankfully, she didn't comment. I had the feeling she'd already caught on to the tension I felt around George, and it would be so embarrassing if she knew the truth. She was perceptive, my boss.

Now, as I finished getting ready for my weekly dinner date with Daphne, it felt like I had an army of ants battling in my stomach. I usually couldn't wait to get out with her and let the worries of the week fall away, yet something was different tonight. I'd been half in love with him since we were kids, but as adults it had gotten a little easier. He lived with a roommate, and I didn't see him every time I saw Daphne anymore. The space helped. The attraction had never gone away, but it was easier to deal with when I avoided him as much as possible.

Daphne had made it clear when we were sophomores that she wasn't happy with our friends always ogling her senior brother. And I didn't blame her, but the message had been clear—hands off. As a result, I'd always felt guilty and kept my long-held attraction for him a secret, because it didn't feel like I had another choice. I knew it was a long time ago, and so much had changed in our lives. But still, I was an Olympic-level overthinker. As time went on, the awkwardness seemed to grow into an insurmountable mountain.

Doing my best to shake off my turbulent emotions, I took in my appearance in the mirror. We always went all-out for our weekly gab-fests, and tonight was no different. I styled my black hair in soft, shining curls down to mid-back, makeup flawless but subtle overall, and the bright red dress I'd chosen matched my lipstick. Black heels, trench coat, and clutch completed the look. If nothing else, at least I looked amazing. The close contour of the dress really made my shape pop, and the shoulder cutouts added that extra something.

Satisfied, I drove through the cobblestone streets of downtown to our favorite sushi place. Its luminescent green sign stood out amongst the statelier surrounding storefronts, and the interior was an elegant design, dimly lit, and dotted with water features. I spotted Daphne in her blue dress already waiting by the sushi display window, checking out the day's specials, and being checked out by the sushi chef's assistant. She was oblivious to her appeal, one of her many endearing qualities.

"Hey, Daph!" I greeted her, and she turned and waved.

"Hey, Bea. You're looking amazing tonight." She swept my outfit with an approving gaze. "Who are you trying to impress?"

I snorted—that was an unfortunate habit of mine this week, it seemed—before answering, "Just trying to keep up with you."

She shook her head in amusement. "Well, we both succeeded in bringing the heat. Now if only there was anyone around here to appreciate that." She glanced around the opulent setting, sadly devoid of eligible men.

My gaze flitted to the wistful look on the sous-chef's face over her shoulder, but I kept my observation to myself. He looked a little young for us.

We took the last two available seats at the long marble bar, so we could watch the chefs prepare our sushi. "So, how's your week been? I know Valentine's is always a crazy week for you at the bakery," she said as she took a sip of her soda.

I shrugged noncommittally. "It's been fine. Busy, but I'm used to that by now."

She sighed. "I wish work would pick up for me. Things are slow right now, giving me plenty of time to agonize over my extremely single status."

Daphne's work as a travel agent gave her great flexibility, but also had major dead seasons. February? Not much travel happening in our area. "I'm sorry Daph, it will pick up come spring. Everyone will be itching to get out of the cold and see some sun."

"I know, I just loathe Valentine's Day. You always have to work the whole day, and I'm left rattling around by myself in an empty apartment trying not to watch all the sappy romance movies on Netflix. Or, if I go out, I'm another desperate single woman alone on V-Day. Not a good look for me, either way." She idly stirred her soda.

"I would be in the same boat if I wasn't working. I'm not exactly rolling in romantic prospects, either." *Because I can't get over your brother long enough to look.*

Engrossed in our conversation, neither one of us noticed that we had company until the sound of a masculine throat being cleared right behind our seats made us jump.

As I turned and saw who it was, embarrassment flooded me from head to toe. Daphne jumped out of her seat to hug her brother, while I wished the ground would open up and swallow me right out of this chair.

"What are you two doing here? You don't even like sushi!" she proclaimed, happiness suffusing her voice.

George shrugged one well-defined shoulder, "Eh, Finn does. He insisted this place was the best in town. And also, that they had stuff that was cooked." He jerked his thumb at Finn, his roommate standing right behind him.

"Weird, we've never seen him in here before. Do you guys want to eat with us? We haven't ordered anything but drinks yet!" she said brightly, pleased to get an unexpected dinner with George.

I cringed inside, loathing the prospect of sitting across from George all night, pretending indifference. But what was my other choice? Refuse to eat with him and make a scene? Nope, I'd have no option except to lock down my feelings for my bestie's sake.

The torture I endure for you, and you don't even know, Daphne.

A server led the four of us to a booth in a quiet back corner next to a multi-colored waterfall. I slid in first, and to my shock and dismay, instead of Daphne, George slid in next to me. I must not have hidden my surprise well, because he gave me a mischievous grin in return.

"Long time, no see. How was your day at work?" he asked.

"It was fine. Busy, as usual." I stopped for a second, and then remembered my manners. "How was yours? Business meeting go okay?"

"Yes, it was good. After the amazing start to my day, I was on top of my game." His warm smile transported me back to our morning run-in, and the sparks once again shimmered between us like fireworks. I quickly looked away, across the table at Daphne and Finn.

The table fell suddenly silent, and Daphne observed us, poised with her straw halfway to her mouth. She slowly lifted it the last few inches and took a long sip. Her look was interminable, and I felt a rush of anxiety at her impending abject disapproval. *Please let it go, please let it go.*

"What amazing start was that?" she asked.

Gah.

"I swung by Sweet Nothings this morning for a cup of coffee and a muffin. Bea here makes the best, as you know." To my everlasting shock, he slid an arm around my shoulders as he said it and gave me a small squeeze.

Heart pounding a mile a minute, I couldn't speak. Daphne's eyes flitted from his arm to my reddened face, and she squinted slightly. "I see. Well, she is the best baker around."

The waiter saved me from having to come up with something intelligent to say by coming over to take our orders. George removed his arm, and I felt both instant sadness and relief at the absence of his warmth.

After we ordered—several sushi rolls to share, and one hibachi plate—Finn and Daphne chatted happily on the other side of the booth, while George and I sat silently.

His low voice—so close to my ear I could feel his breath—made me shudder when he spoke next. "You look stunning tonight, Bea. There's not a man in here who isn't jealous of me right now."

Eyes wide, I turned to see his face mere inches away. "Th-thank you," I spluttered out.

Where is this coming from? Why now, after all these years?

He looked into my eyes, and the warmth of his genuine smile spread through me, tingling up from my toes to the tips of my hair. Feeling like a snake mesmerized by a charmer, I unconsciously leaned in even closer. The air grew thick, the dim lighting wrapped us in a blanket of privacy, and for one second, I blocked everything out and zoned in on George.

"—What do you think, Bea? . . . Earth to Bea!"

My heart-pounding, earth shattering connection with George was doused as if by a bucket of ice water, as reality returned with the sound of Daphne's voice. "Sorry, what?" I whipped my head around to face her again.

"I said, what do you think is better? Spring rolls, or egg rolls? Finn thinks spring rolls, but I think egg rolls."

"Uhm, egg rolls. Spring rolls are too . . . puny," I said, going with the first thing that came to mind.

"Are you okay? You're acting weird tonight." Her look this time was pointed, and I stiffened in my seat.

"Yep, totally fine. I'm exhausted, it was a long day." Guilt flooded me at the white lie. But frankly, I had no idea what to tell her. This new thing with George had thrown me for a loop, and I was confused. Absolutely, panic-inducingly *thrilled*, but confused.

"If you say so," she said, looking unconvinced.

Mercifully, the rest of the dinner was without incident. George went back to normal, polite mode. I pretended the heat radiating off of his leg in the booth next to me wasn't searing a brand on my very being. So, perfectly fine—nothing to see here.

As we all waited for the check, Daphne announced, "I need a visit to the ladies' room. Bea, come with?" She raised her eyebrows and nodded towards the bathroom.

"Sure," I agreed, and George scooted out of the booth and offered me his hand to stand. I tentatively placed my hand in his large warm one and stood. As soon as I could without being too obvious, I snatched my hand away, and pressed it against my thigh instead, where it was safe. The traitorous appendage burned with remembered heat.

For the briefest of seconds, a flash of hurt crossed George's handsome face, and it felt like a dagger to my heart. Now doubly confused, I lowered my eyes to the floor and hurried after Daphne, who was already halfway to the bathroom. The bathroom door swung shut behind us, and loud Asian music pounded through the speakers, making the tiny space feel claustrophobic.

She spun and pinned me with a look, "Okay, what's going on here? Are you and my brother a thing?"

"I, uhm . . . no?" I managed, but she didn't look convinced in the least.

Her jaw dropped. "You and George? *Really*? I didn't think you liked him since, I don't know, high school. What gives?"

I leaned my hip against the bathroom sink and covered my face with my hands. "I don't know, Daphne. You know I've had a crush on him since we were little. But that's it, nothing more. I'd *never* do anything to hurt our friendship, you know that, right? You're the only sister I've got." I look up, and her arms are crossed.

"But still, after all this time, you like him?" is all she asked.

Blush burning my cheeks, I gave a single tiny nod.

"Huh. Well, okay then. Thanks for telling me." She turned and went into the stall without further comment.

I, on the other hand, stood there in shock. That was it? Okay then, thanks for telling me?! Where was the hurt, and anger, and the "Don't lay a finger on my saintly brother, you traitor?"

When she came out and washed her hands, I was still standing right where she left me. She looked me up and down and raised an eyebrow. "Do you need to use the bathroom?"

I shook my head.

"Well, let's get out of here then, before the music gives me a headache. Why is it always so loud in the bathroom?" She pulled the door open, and I followed her out.

I wasn't sure what I was more surprised about; George's possible interest in me, or Daphne's utter lack of response to my lingering feelings for him. Either way, this had already been some night.

We walked back to the secluded corner booth, where George and Finn waited. We each dropped some cash on the bills which had arrived while we were in the ladies' room, and then the four of us shrugged our coats on to brave the night's chill. George helped me into my black trench, and the soft touch of his fingertips on the back of my arm sent a tingle through me.

Daphne chatted with the guys, but I was too in my own head to participate in the conversation as we exited the restaurant. *Was George a possibility, after all? She hadn't been mad, or really reacted at all. Maybe she wasn't okay with it, but was too surprised to say. I'll give it some time to soak in, and ask her outright.*

George held the door for us, ever the gentleman. The gangly kid in a soccer jersey, and the beautiful soul in front of me with kind blue eyes—somehow,

I loved every facet of him, and no other man had measured up to him over the years.

A slight drizzle outside cut short any lingering we might have done, and the frisson of disappointment in my chest was hard to ignore as I walked down the misty sidewalk to my car.

I definitely have to talk to Daphne again. If there's any chance of building something with George, I have to try.

FOUR

Valentine's Day arrived, and I was up before the sun to get the last of the day's orders ready at the bakery. I admittedly took double my usual prep time on my hair and makeup, since I knew I would be spending most of the day riding around with him. I didn't know exactly what was going on between us, but—despite the four a.m. wake up—I wasn't going to look less than spectacular if there was any chance something was starting to build between us. When you wait your entire life for someone to notice you, you can't waste the chance when it finally presents itself.

I shook all thoughts of George out of my head and crossed the still-dark parking lot to the bakery. The lights were already on this morning and Celia had left the door unlocked for me, as she'd opened and started off the baking today. Even though she owned Sweet Nothings, she was still hands-on. There was no leaving a big day like Valentine's Day for someone else to worry about, and I liked that about her.

"Morning Celia," I called to the back.

"Morning Beatrice," she called back, and the merengue music pumping from the kitchen dropped in volume a few notches.

I dropped my purse and keys in the back room, washed up, and grabbed an apron. Celia was in the zone, so other than my initial greeting and a quick side hug, she continued rolling out pastries.

"What are you making?" I asked, as she efficiently cut out dough circles with a ring cutter.

"Another batch of tartlets. I finished the ones we prepped last night, but I got a call from the church, and the ladies ministry ordered a special batch to send all the senior ladies, so we need an extra three dozen." She was a pastry-cutting machine, and when I grew up, I wanted to be her.

"That's nice of them, but really last minute." I grabbed sugar cookie dough from the fridge and started working at the other end of the long prep table.

"It is, but what are you going to do? I'm certainly not telling them no. You know Martha—she's scary when she doesn't get her way," Celia said with an exaggerated grimace.

I chuckled. "You, afraid of someone? Never." We fell into a companionable silence, and I made quick work of the sugar cookies while she knocked out 36 tartlet shells. The rapid beat of merengue kept our hips moving almost as fast as our hands.

Five minutes before seven, we were pulled from our baking trances by a knock at the door.

"I bet that's George—he seems the type to show up early. Will you let him in and grab him some coffee?" Celia suggested, never looking up from the Danish she was now glazing with rapid-fire precision.

"Sure," I said, trying to seem nonchalant. Deep down, I was anything but. While it had been great to get lost in the work this morning, George knocked down all of my walls. I poured a cup of coffee quickly, and then turned to Celia before heading out front. "Celia, are you sure you want me to go on deliveries with him today? It's our busiest day of the year. You're going to need me here."

For the first time all morning, she looked up, brow furrowed. "Of course, I'm sure. I've been running this bakery for more than twenty years; I think I'll be fine for one day. Besides, deliveries are a key part of Valentine's Day success. Now, scoot and take that boy some coffee." Without waiting for a response, she was right back at the Danish pastries.

Hurrying out to the front, coffee in hand, I opened the door to a grinning George leaning casually in the doorway.

"Good morning, you look awfully chipper for someone who got shanghaied into playing delivery boy on the busiest day of the baking year," I observed.

He stepped in the door and gave me a smile so big it made my heart skip a beat. "Well, if I knew you'd be waiting with coffee, I'd show up bright and early every day, not just the busiest day of the year." He accepted the coffee, took a sip, and let out a grateful groan. "Good morning to you, too, by the way."

I gave him a shy smile, but quickly got back to business. "Thanks for coming in. We're getting things ready now to start going in the boxes."

He was hot on my heels as I walked back to the kitchen. "How can I help? Got some sugar cookies for me to work on?"

Celia answered first, all business, "Nope, you can start assembling the boxes, though. Right over there." She nodded to the pile of flat pink boxes in the corner.

"I'm on it!" he said and started folding them up without complaint.

For a few moments, awkwardness lingered as I tried to focus on the next baking task, but Celia's eagle eye didn't miss a thing.

"Bea, let me finish up and you go ahead and start boxing the delivery orders. George has a good pile going over there, and the sooner we get you two out the door with the first batch, the better." She waved to the computer system where the morning delivery orders were queued up.

Shifting gears, I grabbed a box off the top of George's stack, which he was building with machine precision. Trying to ignore his looming presence in the corner, I filled the boxes with fresh baked goodies at a rapid pace and sealed each one with a pink Sweet Nothings sticker. Celia had gone all out with the menu this year, and there were going to be some really happy people today.

My heart squeezed—one day, there would be someone to send *me* a box of goodies. Just not today. We worked in seamless rhythm for the next half hour, until we had an entire cartful of boxes ready to go out on the first morning run. I downloaded the route to my phone, and George headed out the back to load the delivery SUV with boxes. The vehicle was the only part of the business that wasn't pink; it was white with decorative window wraps.

He moved fast in the cold morning, his breath making puffs in the air as he loaded up the back. I stood in the doorway, watching him work. I could never quite put my finger on what it was about him that drew me in like a moth to a flame. I'd known him forever. He was the most genuine, kind man I'd ever met. He loved Daphne with all his heart. And I'd known since the age of seven that if he ever gave me the time of day, I'd be the luckiest girl on the planet.

Now that he finally seemed to notice me, I was in such disbelief that I didn't know what to do, or how to respond. It was going to be a long day. Steeling myself, I stopped staring at his broad back and walked around to the passenger side.

"I've got the route. We're starting on the west side of town and then working our way across today."

"Okay, be right there. I've got to take the cart back in for Celia to refill." He shut the hatch with a click, and I watched in the rear-view mirror as he headed in the back door.

"Just keep it together, Bea. He's always been friendly, and that's it."

He climbed into the driver's seat and cranked the SUV, before turning to me with a smile. "Where to, boss-lady?"

"Schaefer's deli. They ordered all of the individual boxes of sugar cookies to go with their sandwiches today."

"Perfect." He backed out of the spot, and the silence between us wasn't uncomfortable as we drove down the busy streets.

"So, you didn't have to work today? Architect firms close on Valentine's Day now?" I asked, the question niggling at me since he'd agreed to become a delivery man for the day.

He chuckled. "I took the day off. Celia's hard to disappoint."

"Ahh," I answered, unsure what to say to that. It said a lot about him that he'd taken off from his high-paying job to help her, though. *He's such a good man.*

"Plus, how could I resist spending all day with you?" Without looking away from the road, he reached over and gave my hand a squeeze where it rested on the console. To my surprise, he let it linger there, and I gently squeezed his fingers in return.

My stomach did backflips at the realization that I was currently holding hands with George. After a minute, I let out a deep breath that I'd been unconsciously holding. Apparently, we were doing this now.

I peeked over at him out of the corner of my eye, trying to go unnoticed. He was like a living statue, such handsome and chiseled features as he navigated the Savannah traffic with practiced ease. To my chagrin, a few minutes later he had to move his hand to turn on the blinker so we could parallel park out front of Schaefer's deli.

We both piled out and started unloading the tiny individual cookie boxes. Mr. Schaefer had us stack them on the counter next to the register and gave us a nice tip on our way out.

"Give my best to Celia!" he called from behind the counter with a wave.

We hopped back into the car and headed to the next delivery stop. I navigated, and he drove. We fell into a comfortable routine right from the start, and it was nice to see how well we worked together, like a well-oiled machine.

Most of the deliveries were close together, but we hit a longer stretch out of the city.

"So, do you have any big plans tonight?" George asked, pulling me from my silent musings.

"Oh, uhm, no. I don't make plans on Valentine's Day. I work a double every year, and I'm always so tired that I usually go straight home and pass out when it's over." The admission didn't sound too pathetic, I hoped.

"Can't say I blame you there. I'll probably do the same tonight," he said genially.

"No plans for you either? Hot date?" I prodded. If he opened the door, he couldn't blame me for walking through it.

He shook his head. "Nope, not this year. The one I want doesn't seem to be on the market." He glanced at me.

"Oh, so you've got someone in mind?" I said, feeling deflated but trying to keep my voice light.

"Yeah, she's a great girl—kind, smart, beautiful. Really, the total package," he continued.

"She sounds great." I forced a smile. "Why is she off the market?"

"Well, it's kind of complicated. I'm trying to win her over, but it feels like there's an obstacle between us. Sometimes convincing a woman to take a chance is harder than you'd expect." His voice was quiet at the end, sincere.

"I'm sorry to hear that," I murmured, and stared out the window while trying not to look too dejected.

We worked in silence for the rest of the delivery route, until we arrived back at the shop to grab the next cart of deliveries.

"I'm going to run in and use the restroom," I said, avoiding his look. I lingered as long as I could in the bathroom, hoping he'd already be loaded up and waiting by the time I was done. I wanted to avoid any awkwardness with my far-too-perceptive boss. There was a line of customers to the door when I came out, and I felt a stab of guilt for dawdling. *Get the deliveries over with and get back and help Celia. Then you can get some space from George, who's apparently been holding your hand while pining for someone else.*

Anger tried to rise up at the thought, but I squashed it back down. Clearly, he still saw me as his little sister, and I'd been reading far too much into things between us this past week. Otherwise, he wouldn't have told me about the obstacles he was trying to overcome with someone else.

I stormed back out to the car, game face fixed in place. If he could treat me like a sister, I could treat him like a brother. I only had to make it through one day of close proximity, and things would go back to normal. The bakery would once again be my sanctuary, and he could run along and chase his mystery woman. I refused to drive myself nuts thinking about *who she was.* That wasn't a healthy path to go down.

I snatched open the passenger door with a bit too much force, and George's head snapped up. "Everything okay, Bea?"

"Of course, everything's peachy," I said in a cool tone.

"O-kay." There was a long pause. "Are you sure? I'm here and happy to talk if something's bothering you."

I chose to ignore his blatant hinting. "Nope, right as rain. We're heading over to the senior center next. We'll be delivering to the individual rooms, so this one will take a bit."

"Sounds good," he said, and backed out of the space for the second time today.

I reached over and turned on the radio, intent on avoiding any more conversations about dates or plans. Every. Single. Station. Was playing love songs. *Can't I catch a single break? Just one station without a love song.*

I furiously stabbed the next button several times before a masculine, calloused hand reached out and stopped me.

"Bea, please tell me what's wrong. I thought we were having a really nice morning, and you're obviously upset now. Did I do something wrong?" I could hear the hurt and uncertainty in his tone, and it stopped me in my tracks.

"No, George, you didn't do anything wrong. I am sick to death of all this cheery, happy, lovey . . . everything. The longer I'm single, the more I hate

41

Valentine's Day. Like, couldn't ONE station have normal music? Am I going to have to listen to that screamo business to get a break?"

He was quiet while I ranted, driving along and listening. That was one of the things I'd always loved about him—even when I was his little sister's buddy, he always took the time to listen to me, and make me feel like I mattered. *Just not the way I wanted to matter.*

Anger flooded me again, and I went back to jabbing the offensive radio button. This time, he stopped me immediately.

"Let me, I know the perfect station." He quickly punched in a station I'd never listened to before, and the car flooded with upbeat Latin music. All the lyrics were in Spanish.

I looked over, brow furrowed. "What is this?"

He chuckled. "It's probably still a love song, but at least we won't know it. You took French in high school, right?"

"Good memory. Yes, I did." I let the peppy beat wash through me, and some of the tension that had been building since our earlier conversation flooded out. "You're pretty smart, you know that?"

He grinned at me. "Not my first single Valentine's Day, either. You've got to adapt if you want to make it through unscathed."

"Fair enough," I acquiesced. It surprised me that he knew how I was feeling, and had been through the same thing. Somehow, I'd always put him on this pedestal of masculine perfection, when in reality, he was human, too.

We rode, dancing along to the Latin radio station and laughing at our botched attempts to pick up the lyrics all the way to the senior center.

George killed the engine and then looked over at me and grabbed my hand again before I could climb out. "Hey, I know it's a rough day. But, listen—you are going to find someone who's perfect for you. You are too amazing of a person to go through life alone. You have to keep looking. He's probably right in front of you, and you don't even realize it."

Tears at his kindness clogged my throat. "Do you really think so?" I squeaked out.

He gave my hand a squeeze, and I felt the resulting tug in my soul. "I really, *really* do."

"Thanks, George. You're kind of the best." I forced a smile when all I felt like doing was crying. The perfect man was standing right in front of me, and my heart was too stubborn to accept anyone else. *Does he have to be so kind and heart-wrenching at the same time?*

We climbed out and each grabbed a stack of bakery boxes. Each one was labeled with a name and room number. After checking in with Lisa at the front desk, she directed us to the left hallway of residents' rooms. The first door we came to, a nice man in a wheelchair accepted the box of sweets with a toothless smile.

Each resident was pleased as punch to receive the box of goodies, and by the time we headed back to the car for our second stacks of boxes, their cheer had infected me, too. The right hallway looked identical, and we started slowly making our way from door to door with the orders. George took one side, and I took the other.

My third delivery opened his door wearing a silky-looking green paisley bathrobe.

"Hi, Mr. Eulee. I have a delivery for you from the Sweet Nothings bake shop. Happy Valentine's Day." I offered the pink box with a smile, and he took it.

"Who is it from?" he asked, looking through the little window at the bright pink cookies and a strawberry Danish.

"The center arranged for each resident to get one today, as a little surprise."

"That's mighty nice of them," he said, but I could sense his disappointment. Unsure what else to say, I lingered in the doorway. I had quite a few in my stack still to deliver, but it felt wrong to leave him here alone and unhappy.

"Were you expecting something from a special lady?" I asked tentatively.

He shook his head dejectedly. "Oh, no. Old fart like me is long out of the dating game. My Constance has been gone for years, now."

"I'm sorry to hear that. I thought there might have been someone here who caught your eye." My smile was small, and I felt awful for asking.

He shrugged a paisley-clad shoulder and looked over my shoulder with a misty expression. "There are plenty of beautiful gals, but none will ever take the place of my Constance. They broke the mold when they made her. Voice like an angel, but a temper like the devil himself." He cracked a smile at the memory, and I put my hand over my heart.

"Sounds like you two were the real thing. I hope I'm lucky enough to find someone who thinks about me that way, someday."

He focused back on me. "Oh sugar, I'm sure you will. Love is hard, but it's the best thing in the world when it's right. Have you got your eye on a special fella?"

It was my turn to look away, and I caught sight of George down the hall, delivering a box to a little old lady in a purple muumuu and matching curlers. My gaze caught on his brilliant smile, and her fluttered eyelashes in return.

45

"I see. Well, don't wait too long to tell him. Some chances don't come around a second time."

I turned back to find him giving me a knowing look, and blushed. *I'm still waiting for my first chance with him.* "Thanks, Mr. Eulee. I hope you have a nice day."

"I will, sugar. Thanks again." He jangled the box in my direction, and then closed the door. His words, however, bounced around in my head long after we left the senior center.

FIVE

Our third and fourth pickups from the bakery were without incident. We were on our last round of deliveries, finally, as it was nearly dinner time. We'd been trading off who ran the next box up to the door, now that we were in a residential area. This time it was my turn, and I hopped out to grab the next box from the back of the SUV, and noticed one with a post-it on top, note written in Celia's elegant script.

An afternoon pick-me-up for my delivery team!

The little flourishes in pen underneath made me smile. Nothing about Celia was ever plain, down to the last detail. Inside the box sat two muffins, George's favorite blueberry, and a strawberry cheesecake muffin for me. Before running the delivery up to the door, I walked back up front.

"Celia threw in an extra delivery," I said and handed our box to George.

"All right, I knew she liked me," he said with an exaggerated fist pump. He immediately popped the lid and took a whiff.

"Hey, hands off the strawberry one. That's mine." I gave him my I-mean-business glare, to which he responded with raised hands. "Don't act all innocent. We all remember Halloween that one year when you ate all of our Halloween candy after we went to bed. Three bags of candy, and not a *crumb* left for me or Daphne in the morning."

He chuckled. "I paid for that though—my stomach hurt all day. Plus, my dad gave Daphne my dessert every night for a week. I still can't look at taffy to this day." He shuddered at the memory.

Shaking my head, I delivered the box of Valentine's tartlets for this address as fast as humanly possible.

Sliding back into the seat, he handed me the box with my untouched muffin, which I gratefully accepted. I took a bite, and then looked over to see that he had already polished his off.

"You inhaled that thing!" I observed. "What is it with you and blueberry muffins, anyways? You're the only person I know who eats muffins all day. Most people eat muffins first thing in the morning, and by evening they're looking for a sweeter something."

He wrinkled his brow. "Like what, a cupcake or something?"

I finished the bite I was chewing before I answered, as he started driving to our next delivery. "Yeah, exactly. What have you got against cupcakes?"

"Well, for starters, cupcakes are just dressed up, *less* delicious muffins. Think about it; the only thing that separates them is that giant glob of frosting. A muffin has to stand on its own flavor and character, not hide behind a sugary dome of . . . sugar," he argued with surprising conviction.

"You had me going until the 'sugary dome of sugar.' Are you serious? You don't like frosting? You're the first person I've ever met who's actually prejudiced against cupcakes. They're pretty much universally liked."

He chuckled. "I would ask how you know, but you're the expert. What can I say, I'm a baked-goods purist. I like the cake underneath, not the sugary accoutrements." He gave me a wry grin, and I could feel myself being sucked in by his enigmatic allure.

I shook my head dubiously and took another bite of my muffin. *He's not wrong, these are pretty amazing. Just like he is.*

Night began to descend as we hit our last three deliveries. By the time George pulled the delivery SUV back into the employees' lot behind the bakery, it was twilight. The antique streetlights cast a soft glow, highlighting the puffs of our breath as we climbed out of the SUV for the last time today.

I stretched, surprisingly stiff from the long day in and out of the car. George walked around to my side in time to catch the end of my overhead arm stretch.

"Need a back rub? I'm feeling pretty sore myself." He smiled and rubbed his left shoulder with his right hand and made an exaggerated pained face.

"Yeah, I forgot you're a fancy architect who's used to hanging out in a plush office all day, drawing things." I smiled while I teased him.

He gripped his chest as if he'd been shot and staggered back a step. "Oh, she doesn't like muffins or architects? I'm oh for two!"

"Oh, shut up. You know I like you, *and* muffins. How could I not?" I punched him lightly on the shoulder. His eyes locked with mine, and heat built between us. My heartbeat increased in tempo until it was nearly as fast as the merengue music Celia was so fond of.

"Is that so?" he asked, an edge to his tone. He took a half step closer, closing the distance between us. Being this close to him felt like I was a moth inching closer to a flame. I might get burned up, but I'd enjoy every second I spent basking in his warmth. His masculine scent reached my nose, and I had to stop myself from leaning in closer for another whiff.

"Of course. What's not to like?" I kept my tone light, unsure where he was going with this. He'd told me about the girl he was after earlier, and yet here we were, sparks flying with abandon.

George leaned in, so close our foreheads were nearly touching. He lifted a single finger and trailed it down my cheek, soft as a whisper to the corner of my lips. "You're gorgeous, Bea. Absolutely, heart-stoppingly, perfect."

My mouth dropped open. "What?" My brain chose that unfortunate moment to take a leave of absence, and that was the only word that came to mind.

He leaned back just a hair and lifted his gaze from my lips back to my eyes. "You heard me. You're stunning, and I had a blast spending the day with you. I would really like to do it again sometime if you'd be willing."

I am not proud of how long I gaped at him before my brain started forming words again. "But, what about the other woman? The one you're trying to get things going with, but there's an obstacle . . ." I trailed off as it suddenly clicked into place.

Oh, my Lanta. Oh, my stars. Oh! My! Goodness! Bea, you blind bird!

His smile spread slowly, like a blossom bending in a summer breeze as he watched me connect the dots. "Bea, surely you knew I was talking about *you*, right?" He leaned forward again, but this time his lips, soft and warm and firm all at once, connected with mine in a tender kiss.

Time slowed to a stop, and this single moment with George consumed me, body and soul. Heat blossomed in my chest, and the world tilted on its axis. This was George, the man I'd been longing for my whole life, and in this moment, everything clicked into its perfect place. My heartbeat pounded in my ears when he pulled back, a secret smile on his lips. I touched my own lips, in shock that he felt the same way about me that I did about him.

"I know you haven't seen me in a romantic light in the past, but I hoped that you might be willing to consider the possibility of more between us," he whispered, breath mingling with mine.

"I had no idea you would want that. I thought you saw me as another little sister. You've never shown any interest before, even after all this time . . . Why now?" I hesitated to ask, but a part of me deep down had to know.

It was his turn to snort. "Bea, are you serious? The summer you turned seventeen, you and Daphne got matching red polka-dot bikinis, and you almost gave me a heart attack the first time I saw you in it."

I blushed, remembering the exact bathing suits he was referring to. I'd coerced Daphne into buying it so I wouldn't be alone in the tiny suit. "You didn't act like you noticed." *And the only reason I'd bought that ridiculous suit was to get you to notice.*

"Yeah, because, the year before, Daphne threatened me to within an inch of my life if I ever tried to date you, and I quote, 'steal her bestie.'" He made finger quotes in the air to illustrate his point.

Cold water flooded my veins at the key reminder of what was standing between us. There was no way I was going to lose my best friend, and he'd just confirmed that Daphne wasn't okay with a relationship between George and me.

My heart fell to my feet and I looked down, unsure what to say. My heart, soaring from his kiss a moment before, felt like it had crashed into a best-friend-shaped cliff. I had hoped to talk to her about pursuing something with George, and here we were, on the brink of what I wanted so desperately, only to have him tell me she'd already forbidden it.

"Hey, what's wrong? Have I misread you? If you're not into me, you can say so. I won't push things if you're not interested, or make them awkward." He leaned back, looking worried, and reached out to brush my arms lightly with both hands. Electricity surged through me even at the tender touch, but the guilt wouldn't ease up.

I looked up, touched by the sincerity in his blue eyes. The darkness couldn't hide the emotion there, and my heart squeezed painfully.

"No, you didn't misread anything. I've been into you since the first time I saw you in a soccer jersey, when I was seven."

The grin he gave me nearly took the breath from my lungs with its intensity. "Seriously? And you never told me? That's amazing, Bea." He wrapped me up in a spontaneous hug, and for the briefest moment, I let myself sink into his chest, and squeezed him back, hard. I didn't allow myself to linger, though, and pulled back. Everything inside of me protested, but it was the only option.

"It's not amazing, George. You just said Daphne warned you off and told you not to date me." I ran a frustrated hand through my black curls. "I know she's your sister, but she's my best friend in this world, George. I can't go behind her back and date her brother, no matter how much I want to. We can't pursue this, not if Daphne's not okay with it." I crossed my arms across my chest protectively, hating the words even as they left my mouth.

"Bea, we were teenagers when she said that! I am sure now that we're adults, she won't care. It's not the same now as it was back then." He put both hands on my shoulders and drew me slowly back to his chest.

I was suddenly overcome with sadness, and tears stung my eyes. Why was it that even when there was finally something between us, I still had to push him away? I couldn't see any chance of it working out if Daphne was against our relationship.

"I don't know, George, Daphne isn't one to change her mind. She guessed that I still had a crush on you, back at the sushi restaurant. She didn't seem happy." My words came out muffled against the fabric of his shirt, but he heard me anyways.

"Why do you say that? Maybe she was surprised and needs some time to get used to the idea." He rested his chin on my head, and we fit together like two halves of a perfect puzzle. The observation made my heart do a backflip in my chest.

I forced myself to pull back, even though each inch of separation from him killed me a little bit more.

"I'm sorry, George. I don't think so. As much as I love you, have always loved you, I won't screw up my relationship with Daphne. She's been there for me through everything, and I could never hurt her like that."

He frowned, and looked like he wanted to argue, but I cut him off. My heart couldn't take any more. "I'm sorry, George, I need to get inside and finish out my shift. Thank you for everything today. It was an amazing day." My voice cracked on the last sentence, and I tucked my head and all but ran towards the back door. If I didn't get some distance from him now, I might give in to his persuasion, and lose my best friend in the process.

"Bea, please wait. Don't go, let's talk this through!" His voice was pained, and I felt my heart shatter.

Even though my heart was crumbling further to pieces with each step away from George, I forced myself to do the right thing. *I just wish it didn't feel so wrong.*

Six

I t had been a restless, sleepless night. I'd tossed and turned all night long thinking about the day's events. Spending all day in close proximity to George had been a sweet kind of torture. There was real chemistry between us now. Plus, that kiss . . . What was I supposed to do about that? What would *Daphne* make of that? I didn't want to lose my best friend over a relationship with her brother, even if he was the only man I'd ever had feelings for.

I scrubbed at my sandy eyes, and climbed out of bed, determined to find something to take my mind off of George. The first day off I'd had in weeks, I took a leisurely shower and then decided to make some breakfast. I wandered to my little apartment kitchen and rummaged through the fridge, but none of the usual breakfast suspects sounded good. My eyes fell on a pint of blueberries, and an idea struck.

I quickly set to work baking and lost myself in the familiar process. Preheat oven, gather ingredients, prep pans—the rhythm soothed me, freed my mind to think. As I cracked eggs and stirred the simple batter, it became clear to me that I couldn't continue on as I had been. I'd kept up the status quo for years, silently pining for George, and ignoring any other man that came along. Somehow, they never quite measured up.

But after yesterday, after that amazing kiss, I couldn't do it anymore. I didn't have it in me at the moment to examine too closely *why* exactly I couldn't. But it became crystal clear to me as I scooped the batter into the oversized brown cupcake liners—I had to talk to Daphne.

I slid the pan into the oven and leaned against the stove. Every step away from George the night before had felt like my heart was being ground to dust. We had a genuine connection, and I couldn't keep that from Daphne anymore. But how did you tell your best friend that you were in love with her brother?

I puttered around the small kitchen, washing up the mixing bowl and utensils I'd used to make the batter. This place was small, and a little dated. But it was my first place that was completely my own, and I could afford the rent easily on my bakery salary.

I had just dried and put away my glass mixing bowl when I heard my phone buzz on the counter. I picked it up, and it was a text from Daphne.

Daphne: Hey B, you home?

Bea: Yep, making breakfast. What's up?

Daphne: I'm in the neighborhood with coffee, mind if I swing by?

Bea: Of course not, come on over.

Not even two minutes later, there was a swift knock at the door. I nervously crossed to the front door and let Daphne in.

"Hey Daph, what are you up to this morning?" I asked, as I led her back to the kitchen.

She hopped up on a bar stool and slid me a paper to-go cup from the coffee shop down the street before taking a sip of hers. "Well, I didn't hear from you after your shift last night, and I figured we could catch up."

I sighed and picked up the cup. "Yeah, it was a long day. I'm sorry I didn't call, I was too . . ." I trailed off, unsure where to even begin. The oven timer beeped, and I grabbed a puffy cerulean oven mitt to pull out the muffin tin.

"Those smell amazing," Daphne observed as the scent wafted over to her before abruptly changing the subject on me. "So, I had an interesting chat with George last night."

I froze, muffin tin on the stovetop, my back still to her. Taking a deep breath, I slowly turned back around. "Oh, yeah?"

"Yeah. Seems he had some things he wanted to discuss with me. About this girl he kissed last night."

My heart squeezed in my chest. Her face was unreadable as she sipped her coffee, and I rushed to explain. "Daphne, I was planning to call you today, I just didn't even know where to begin to explain—"

She held up a hand and smiled, cutting off my frantic blather. "Girl, we've known each other since we were kids. I already asked if you liked George. We're good."

"I know, we just talked about it, but I know you don't approve, and I cut it off. I— Wait, what?" It took me a moment to catch up to what she'd said.

Her smile widened. "Bea, you're not as subtle as you think. I love you, but you have a crappy poker face. Seriously, it's a good thing you're a baker, because if you tried to be a hostage negotiator, those poor people would die." She took a sip of her coffee.

A strangled laugh escaped me, and I shook my head at her peculiar brand of honesty. She kept me on my toes, that's for sure. "So, you're cool with me and George . . . dating?" I asked one more time, to be one hundred percent certain.

She rolled her eyes. "Yes, gracious. It took you two long enough to figure out you liked each other, though. Honestly, you've both been dancing around it since that year with the red polka dot bikinis. By the way, I am still salty about the fact that I had to wear that ridiculous thing too, and I don't have a hottie to show for it." She pointed an accusing finger in my direction.

"I'll make it up to you. Want to try again? We can get new bikinis and go to the community pool." I waggled my eyebrows at her suggestively, and she shook her head emphatically.

"It's February, in case you'd forgotten. I'm not interested in becoming a human popsicle, so, no thanks. But I'll think of some way you can make it up to me, don't you worry about that."

Relief at how easy and normal our banter was—even though the truth was all out on the table about George—flooded me like a wave. The wave, however, abruptly crashed me right back into how I'd left things with George the night before, and I leaned my elbows on the counter and put my head in my hands.

"Hey, what's wrong? Aren't you supposed to be happy right now that you have the coolest BFF in existence?" Daphne prodded.

I groaned before answering. "Daphne, I'm glad you're cool and all, but I think I may have ruined things with George before they even got going."

"Uhm, how do you think you ruined it, exactly?"

I looked up, sorrow on my face. "Well, last night, we kissed." She made a face, and I hurried to continue. "But only once, and I told him I couldn't pursue anything with him, without your okay. I told him I wasn't willing to risk our friendship for a relationship with him." The words came out in a tangled rush, and my heart was in my throat. *Now he's going to think I don't care about him, but that couldn't be further from the truth.*

"Ha! That's right, big brother. She picked me!" Daphne pumped an enthusiastic fist in the air and did a little dance on the barstool.

"Would you cut it out? This is not helping. I finally got a shot with George, and I screwed it up! What am I going to do?"

"Bea, you are way overthinking this. He's a man, and he's been half in love with you since he was sixteen. You literally baked a fresh batch of blueberry muffins this morning, which are his favorite of all time, because he's a weirdo." She gestured at the cooling muffins, forgotten behind me in the tin. "All you need to do is show up at his house with a few of those, and bing-bang-boom, you're together." She made an exploding gesture with her hands.

"You think muffins are going to convince him to give me another shot, after he kissed me and told me how he felt, and I pushed him away and told him I didn't want to risk it?" I stated, unconvinced.

Daphne nodded, sure of herself.

"Well, I guess it couldn't hurt to take a peace offering and try to talk to him." I turned the idea over in my mind, and I couldn't come up with a better one. "I should call first."

She rolled her eyes. "Bea, for Pete's sake, just go over there, knock on the door, and tell him how you feel."

"What if he's not home? It's Saturday, he could be out."

"You sit on the front porch with a basket of muffins and think about how you're not going to screw this up again. Come on, let's get you dressed. Maybe something red, so he'll remember the bikini."

I groaned again. "You're impossible, Daphne."

"You know you love me," she said over her shoulder as she headed to my room. And she was right, I did.

SEVEN

I took a deep breath, steeling myself as I climbed the front steps of the cute yellow house where George lived. The entire drive over I'd rehearsed in my head what I'd say when he opened the door. That I'd talked to Daphne, and I really liked him, and if he would give us another shot, I thought we could be great together.

I paused in front of the screen door and slowly exhaled through my nose. Yoga breathing was doing nothing for me today, so I decided to go for it. I lifted a shaking hand and knocked on the door. Standing there, holding a half-dozen muffins in my cream-colored dress—not red, much to Daphne's chagrin—was the longest minute of my life. An entire marching band paraded through my stomach before I heard footsteps approach the door. Then, the drum line started to play.

I tried not to look nervous as it swung open, to reveal Finn on the other side. Slightly deflated, I asked, "Oh, hi, Finn. Is George home?"

"No, but he should be back any minute. He just ran out to do an errand. Come on in, you can wait for him." He stood back and made a flourishing gesture towards the living room.

"Thank you, that would be great." I walked in and stood awkwardly by the couch, still holding the muffins.

He walked up beside me, and finally noticed the box. "What have you got there?"

"Some blueberry muffins for George. I brought extras, so I'm sure he'll be willing to share," I added, not wanting to seem rude.

"Are you sure about that? Because I'm pretty sure he *won't*." He eyed the box longingly. "If you want, you can put them in the kitchen."

"Good idea, thanks." I wandered into the kitchen, leaving behind a distracted Finn whose phone had just rung.

Their kitchen was small, but tidier than one might expect for two bachelors living alone. Decorated in forest green accents, it definitely had a masculine feel. I set the box of muffins on the counter and turned to find an agitated-looking Finn standing in the kitchen entryway.

"Hey, I have to run. George should be here any minute, so you can wait here for him. If he asks . . . tell him something came up, and I'll be back later." He shot two finger guns at me and left abruptly, without waiting for a response.

I frowned, uncertain what to do. On the one hand, I wanted to see George, but I didn't want him to think I was some stalker who'd snuck into his house. Finn's abrupt departure didn't leave me many options, unfortunately.

I searched all around the kitchen for a notepad and pen. In the last drawer I tried, I finally found one.

I scratched out a quick note, telling him I'd dropped by and to please call me when he got home. I tore it off, folded it up on top of the muffin box, and tucked the notepad back away. Just as I was walking out of the kitchen, the sound of voices on the porch rooted me to the spot.

George's familiar voice reached me through the door, along with an unfamiliar female voice. My heart fell to my feet.

Is he really coming in right now with another woman, after he just kissed me last night? Disappointment flooded me but was quickly replaced by horror. *Oh my word, he is going to come in with this woman and find me in his kitchen like a frozen creeper if I don't get out of here!*

I was frozen like a love-struck idiot—my half-cocked muffin-delivery plan completely botched—listening to the man of my dreams chat up another woman. Love had finally made me lose it. There was no other explanation for this situation.

I frantically looked around for another exit. No back door. *Shoot, what am I going to do?*

My eyes landed on the cracked bedroom door right off the living room, and the nice, waist-high window I could see.

Crouching down, I hurried through the door, pulled it to and winced as the hinges creaked. *Please don't notice, please don't notice.*

I heard the front door open, and George's voice carried down the hall. "Here, Cindy, have a seat on the couch and I'll be right back." I heard the clink of keys hitting a bowl, and his steps echoed down the short hallway.

Forcing myself to keep moving, I crossed to the window, undid the latch and shoved the window upwards. It popped and creaked as it bumped upwards in the track, and I internally cursed the creaky old house. George's footsteps faded behind the blood rushing in my ears as I looked out the window to the sad, nearly bare bushes right below. Cursing my decision to listen to Daphne and wear a dress, I tossed one leg out the window. *Better scraped up than caught.*

Before I could get my other leg out the window—thank you, stupid pencil dress—to my horror, the bedroom door swung open, and in walked George.

His eyes swung and landed on me, half-in, half-out the window with my knees trussed like a Thanksgiving turkey by my clinging ivory skirt, and confusion crossed his handsome features.

"Bea, what in the world?"

"Oh, my God," was all I got out before I leaned too far back, and promptly fell out of the window and into the sad bush beneath. I lay there, stunned—being jabbed by twigs in too many places to count—until George's head popped out of the window above me.

"Bea, are you okay? What are you doing climbing out of Finn's window?" His sudden appearance snapped me out of my shocked stupor, and I cartwheeled out of the bush like a panicked starfish. He leaned out and extended an arm, as if to help me stand up.

I backed away, cheeks burning and heart pounding. "I was just leaving. Go back to your guest!" I turned and made for the side gate, limping slightly from my fall. Humiliation was hot on my heels, and no way was I outrunning it in my current state.

"Bea, wait!" he shouted, but I ignored him and focused all my efforts on escaping the mortifying situation.

I cleared the gate and made it past the front porch nearly to the street before he caught me.

"Bea, would you stop?" He grabbed my arm, and spun me to face him before releasing me.

"I'm sorry, George, I was just leaving." I gestured to my car, parked across the street. So *close, and yet, so far.*

"Bea, I don't want you to leave. I want you to tell me what's going on," he said sternly.

Blushing furiously, I dropped my gaze to his shoes. "I came by to talk to you about last night, and Finn let me in and then left. I wrote you a note to call me and was about to leave when I heard you coming in. With *Cindy.*"

I looked up, to see the lady in question hovering in the front door with an amused look on her face.

He rubbed his hand over his face in exasperation. "It didn't occur to you to just wait and say hello? Cindy is Finn's ex-girlfriend. She cornered me at the grocery store and followed me home to try to catch

Finn. I called and told him she was on her way, which is probably why he bailed on you."

My jaw dropped. "I . . . don't even know what to say to that."

"I'm going to have words with that idiot when he gets home about why he didn't tell me that you were waiting for me," he added, annoyance coloring his tone.

"I'm so sorry, George. I wanted a chance to talk to you about everything that happened last night, and then I got spooked. I thought that you'd already found somebody new, and I didn't want you to think I was some crazy person hanging out in your kitchen when you weren't home." I hid my face in my hands, embarrassment refusing to subside.

"Wait, why were you in the kitchen?"

I peeked over the edge of my hands at his face, relieved that he wasn't angry, at least. "Well, I brought you muffins. I left them in the kitchen."

A grin split his handsome face. "You brought me muffins?" He took a step closer, and leaned in toward me. "That seems like something you might do for your boyfriend. *Especially* if they're blueberry."

Breathless at his sudden proximity and the heat radiating off of his chest, I shook my head. "Well, I talked to Daphne this morning."

"Oh, really? Interesting conversation?" He reached forward as if he was going to stroke my hair, but instead plucked a dried twig out of it.

Just when you think it can't get any more humiliating.

"I told her about last night, about what happened between us." I looked down again, the fear that I'd ruined my shot with him overwhelming everything else in that moment.

He put one finger under my chin and lifted it until my eyes locked with his. "And did she tell you that her brother had already filled her in on the fact that he's crazy about you?"

I gave him a small nod.

"Did she also tell you she gave said brother the green light to woo you like a fourteenth-century knight in shining armor?"

I furrowed my brow. "No, not that part . . . She suggested that I come over and talk with you and bring you muffins." I paused, processing this new information. "Although, she *was* rather sure of herself when she told me you'd give me another shot."

He shook his head in derision. "That's Daphne, always one to bury the lead."

He reached up and smoothed an errant black curl back from my face. Luckily, no more sticks from his attack bush got in the way.

His eyebrows drew down in a smoldering expression. "Bea, I have a very important question. But first, I have a little something for you."

"Okay," I said, palms damp and stomach knotted with nervous anticipation.

He took my hand and led me back up the front steps. Cindy, purse in tow, waved and passed us on her way out.

"I'll come back by and see Finn later." She hit the sidewalk and didn't look back.

George didn't comment, just led me back to the bedroom doorway, and bent down to pick up a pink bakery box that I hadn't noticed him carrying before, from my position on the windowsill.

"It sounds like you and I had the same idea today." He opened the box, and handed it to me, so the contents were facing me.

Inside were nestled eight heart-shaped sugar cookies, but instead of the usual sparkly sugar topping, he'd had them piped so they spelled out, "BEA MINE?"

"Oh, George, I love them!" I looked up and saw his dazzling smile. "Did Celia make these for you?"

He nodded. "Funny story, actually. I went in to ask her to make me something for you, and she already had that sitting behind the counter, waiting. I think she might be psychic."

He took the box from my hands, and set it on the kitchen counter, right next to my box of blueberry muffins. But rather than investigate those, he turned to face me, and took a step closer, edging me toward the refrigerator. His voice dropped low, barely above a whisper, and he leaned in so close I could feel the next words brush against my cheek. "There's just one thing I need to ask you, Bea."

I shivered at the sensation of his breath, his lips tantalizingly close. "Anything, George. What is it?" I said, caught in his alluring gaze, with my heart galloping in my chest. The memory of our first kiss on my lips begged to be repeated—I knew how soft his lips were now, and I needed to feel them against mine like I needed my next breath.

"I know it's a day late, but would you be my valentine?" His expression was serious, but the corner of his lip quirked up in a hint of a smile.

"Hmm, I don't know. Punctuality is important, after all. Maybe next year," I teased, trailing a finger down his toned chest. He was looking particularly good today in a dark green Henley, a fact I'd overlooked earlier in my haste to escape. Now, I took the moment to drink him in. His golden hair was slightly mussed, and those deep blue eyes sparkled with happiness at our light banter. He was close—and irresistibly magnetic—and I wanted a million more moments with him, just like this one. My eyes fell to his lips once more, slightly parted now and oh-so-inviting.

"I'll hold you to that," he said, and closed the last tiny distance between us. His lips met mine, and all thoughts fled. I was consumed by his warm, masculine scent and the flood of electricity engulfing my body. He threaded his hands into my hair and I tipped my head back to deepen the kiss. I rested a hand on his strong chest, lost in the moment.

While I'd never been a girl who loved Valentine's Day, I was already looking forward to it next year . . . with him.

EIGHT

Epilogue

SIX WEEKS LATER

Daphne and I climbed the steps to George's front porch, each carrying a dish for game night. The guys had wanted to watch baseball and get pizza delivered, but had compromised on the food when they heard we'd bring baked mac-and-cheese, and Daphne's famous squash casserole. They were grilling burgers and had picked up dessert from the shop earlier today.

We knocked, and George greeted us a moment later, giving each of us a kiss on the cheek. Finn was in the living room behind him, soda in hand, shouting at the TV. "Come on, ump! Get it together!"

I snorted. "Are we going to have to listen to him yell all night? That's not a very romantic date."

Daphne interjected. "This is not a date. A date would imply that I was also here to date someone, and there's no way in heck I'm getting near Finn." She shook a finger at us to emphasize her point before turning to take off her shoes.

George shrugged one shoulder. "He probably will keep it up all night, but I'll make it up to you. What do you say tomorrow night, we go out for dinner—just the two of us?" He leaned in and dropped his voice to a heated whisper. "I've been thinking about you all day. Those eyes, that smile—it's been way too long since I've seen you. Pure torture." His fingers trailed along my jawline, and left a delicious tingle in their wake.

"Let the record show that one whole day apart is too long," I teased him, but secretly I loved knowing that he was just as wrapped up in me as I was in him. I'd always been a perpetual overthinker, but George was slowly building my trust in his feelings for me.

"Exactly. I'm glad we're on the same page here." Closing the gap between us, he gave me a much better kiss. My hand fluttered up to the back of his neck and my fingertips wrapped into the strands of his short blonde hair of their own accord. A long moment later we finally parted when an unfamiliar masculine voice interrupted us. I stepped back, a blush coloring my cheeks.

"Terribly sorry to bother you, but I was going to throw the burgers on and can't get the grill to light. I tried to ask Finn, but he waved me off." His British accent was the first thing I noticed, followed quickly by his tall, well-muscled build and chiseled jaw with a five o'clock shadow.

"Sorry man, I'll come help. It's a little tricky, but I can show you." George clapped him on the shoulder, and they headed for the grill.

"Who was that? I've never seen him before," I said, looking over at Daphne who was following his exit with an intent gaze.

"I don't know, but I intend to find out," she said, a gleam in her eye. "Did you hear that accent? I'd like him to read me a bedtime story. Hot *dang*."

I snorted at her enthusiasm, but I couldn't blame her. You didn't exactly find a man like that around every corner in this town. She passed me her casserole dish and trailed behind George and the handsome stranger. "Don't do anything I wouldn't do!" I called after her, but she waved me off.

This is going to be interesting.

The End

NINE

Bless Your Heart

BONUS SHORT STORY

I tried not to tap my foot impatiently as the cotton-topped little old lady in front of me in the checkout line slowly loaded her groceries on the belt. Apparently Express Lane didn't apply to the patrons, just the number of items. Although, on second look, she'd packed more than 15 items on the belt, too.

Pasting on my best smile, I asked her, "Ma'am, can I help you load up your things?"

"Why, yes, dear. How lovely of you to offer!" she said as she ambled towards the front of the line to pay.

"It's no problem, happy to help," I said, and quickly finished loading her very full grocery cart onto the belt. Just then, a handsome stranger joined the line behind me, carrying a bouquet of red roses and a box of chocolates. Somebody in this town is going to be thrilled tonight. I took him in from his thick, dark hair and chocolate eyes, to a well-defined chest, fitted jeans, and dark leather shoes. I snapped my gaze back up to see him give me a smile that could melt a popsicle, and a nod before he assessed the reality that this lane would not be moving quickly.

"So dear, are you married?" The lady asked, inspecting my clearly bare left hand. I reached up and tucked a strand of auburn hair behind my ear to remove the offending digit from her scrutiny.

"No ma'am, not yet." I forced a smile, despite my inward loathing of the question. I got it; I was thirty. Most of the women I went to high school with were well past married and on to their second or third child. However, Prince Charming had yet to show himself. So there I was: thirty, unmarried, and no kids in sight—much to my mama's chagrin.

It's not like I wouldn't love to find someone—if not to marry, then at least to have a serious relationship with—but I have always struggled with putting myself out there. Being vulnerable is hard. Plus in this town, once that first blush of your twenties has passed, everyone started treating you like a bug under a microscope, and any hint of romance had the tongues wagging.

"Well, you aren't getting any younger. You look at least twenty-five. In my day, you'd be considered a spinster by now!" She pulled out a checkbook and pen, which saved me from being forced to answer.

I turned to the side to check out the magazines, intent on not drawing any more of her attention, only to spot Mr. Handsome with a barely concealed grin, having clearly seen the whole thing. My face colored instantly. Why must my humiliation be in front of the hottest man I've seen in a month? Just why?

He leaned in conspiratorially and whispered, "If it makes you feel any better, I'm sure you've got plenty of child-bearing years ahead of you."

"Ha-ha, aren't you hilarious." I shot him a glare. Handsome or not, there's a line.

He stuck his hand out to shake, "Tucker Jones. And, yes, some people say I am," and flashed me a cocky grin.

I reluctantly shook his hand, "Marlie."

"Nice to meet you, Marlie. I know it's forward of me, seeing as we just met and all, but do you have plans tonight?"

I glanced down pointedly at the flowers and chocolates, which were clearly intended for someone, before answering, "Yes, actually, I'm afraid I do have plans tonight." My baby sister's wedding rehearsal. Jenny's a girl who's never had an issue putting herself out there. Twenty-three, and she'd already blown through an impressive list of boyfriends before she committed to John.

"Honey, when a man that tall and good-looking asks you out, you say, yes! Bless your heart, I think we found the problem." The little old lady tsked and took her receipt from the cashier and slowly pushed her cart away.

"You have a nice day now, Mrs. Lindy," the cashier said to her retreating form.

Tucker chuckled behind me as I chucked my bottle of nail polish on the belt and shoved a five-dollar bill at the cashier. She took it all in with an amused expression and popped her bubble gum loudly, in no hurry to end my nightmare of shame.

Dear ground, please swallow me now.

"Have a nice day, now," she drawled.

I nodded abruptly and fled out the door, eager to hide my flaming face. Digging in my purse, I pulled out my keys and climbed into my SUV. I started it up and threw it in reverse, only to hear an odd thwump-thwump as I back out of the space. What in the world is that?

Tossing it in park, I jumped back out and walked around the car to see if I could find what caused the noise.

"You've got to be kidding me. Really?" I looked up at the sky, as if to question the heavens directly. "Today of all days. Ugh," I groaned.

"Don't tell me the car asked if you're single, too. What is the world coming to?" A now-familiar voice startled me from the side, and I spun on my heels to face none other than Tucker Jones, his gifts now tidily bagged.

"No, thank you very much. My tire is flat." I pointed to the offending piece of rubber, tempted to kick it. I still might, once he leaves.

He set the bag down on the pavement and walked over, "It sure is. Let me take a look."

"Oh, no! I can't put you out. I'll call my dad. Really, you should go," I urged him, but he ignored me. Dropping down to one knee, he looked around the flat tire.

After a moment of me watching him tensely, he let out a whistle, "You picked up a screw straight through the sidewall. I'm afraid you're going to need a new tire. Do you have a spare?" He stood, dusting off his hands before he looked to me for an answer.

"Yes, but really, it's fine. I can just wait for my dad to get here!" I tried to wave him off, but he was a man on a mission.

"It's probably in the back." He popped open my hatch, and made quick work of the cover, exposing the spare. He did a quick inventory of the tools, and then pulled out what he needed and went to work.

We stood in silence while he pumped on the miniature jack handle for at least a minute, and I just watched his arm muscles move up and down. The car barely budged despite his efforts. The fact that he dwarfed the tiny thing made him look ridiculous, but he didn't seem fazed in the least. I watched in fascination as a single bead of sweat rolled down his tanned neck, taunting me as it slipped inside his shirt collar. I could see myself kissing that same path, down to what has to be a drool-worthy chest underneath.

I mentally shook myself, and finally thought of something coherent to say. "So, do you just go around changing women's flat tires all the time? Isn't someone expecting you?"

His brow furrowed, but he didn't stop pumping on the jack when he answered, "Why would someone be expecting me, exactly?"

I gestured to the bag, forgotten on the ground, "Well, you bought those for somebody. She's probably expecting you, right?"

Understanding dawned on his tanned face, "Ahh, yes. Great-aunt Celia is in fact expecting me. I've been out of town for a while, and I always bring her a little something when I visit. My uncle died about five years ago now, so she gets lonely when I'm away on business."

Well, it's official. I'm a heel. God, the man had just met me and was changing my tire, meanwhile I was ribbing him about the flowers and chocolates for his widowed great-aunt.

"That is really sweet of you to think of her," I said, contrition in my tone. "Not many people take time to visit their older relatives these days."

The wry grin he gave me sent a flutter through my stomach, which I chose to ignore. "Aunt Celia is a hoot. I enjoy the visits as much as she does." He removed my sad, deflated tire and rolled it to the back of the car where the spare waited.

"Are you sure I can't help you with that? It looks heavy." I watched as he picked it up and settled it in place as if it were in fact, not heavy and awkward to hold. His forearms flexed enticingly as he started tightening the lug nuts and I swallowed, mouth suddenly dry.

"Nah, wouldn't want you to get your hands dirty for your plans this evening." He winked, and a blush engulfed my face.

"I really do have plans that I can't break. I'm sorry, I wasn't trying to blow you off." I said, as guilt hit me for being dismissive before.

"It's all right, maybe another time." He quickly worked the jack back down, and then checked the tightness of my spare. With a self-satisfied nod, he brushed his hands off on his dark jeans before looking back at me. "Ok, you should be good to go. I'll pop this in the back here. That spare isn't full sized, so you'll need to get a new tire as soon as you can. It's not safe to drive on a donut too long."

"Thank you so much, Tucker. I really do appreciate it. Here we just met, and I can't believe you were so kind as to help me out," I said, unsure where to go from here. While I wished we could go back in time to that moment where he'd asked me what I was doing later, that chicken had already flown the coop.

"Don't worry about it. My daddy raised me to always help people out when I can. I hope you and I run into each other again sometime." He picked up his bag, gave me one last nod, and then walked away. I circled around to my driver's-side door and pre-

tended not to watch as he climbed into a jacked-up
red pickup truck two rows over.

After a quick trip to the tire shop, I rushed to get
dressed for the rehearsal dinner. I didn't have time
to apply my new nail polish, but there was always
tomorrow. At least I felt confident in my strapless
black dress; it hugged my curves just right, and
showed off my porcelain skin. Not that there will be
anyone to impress tonight. I slipped on my strappy
black heels and hurried out the door, knowing I
would probably be a few minutes late despite my
best efforts. Having a good excuse wouldn't stop my
mama from getting after me for holding things up.

I pulled in at the small country church, and the
parking lot was so full it looked like Jenny had in-
vited the entire family to the rehearsal dinner. That
meant I was probably in for a night full of, "When are
you going to catch a man like your baby sister did?"
Great. My favorite way to spend a Friday night.

Making my way up the steps, I slipped through
the back doors of the sanctuary and stopped for a

moment to let the blasting AC wash over my already sticky skin. As suspected, most of our extended family and John's were taking up the pews. Jenny and her three other bridesmaids stood off to the side and spotted me immediately.

"Marleen Delilah Abernathy! Where have you been? We were supposed to start fifteen minutes ago. You missed all the partner swapping!" she scolded, voice rising at the end.

"I'm sorry, Jenny. I got a flat tire and had to get it changed out. I'm here now, and I'll walk with whoever is left," I said, trying to placate her.

"Well," she gave a dainty sniff, "You are my favorite sister, so I have done you a favor, whether or not you'll appreciate it."

I knew I shouldn't ask, because, knowing Jenny, I wouldn't like the answer. But I couldn't stop myself. "What do you mean, 'a favor?'"

"Why, she gave you the best groomsman, of course," Joanne pouted.

"Gawd, he is a tall drink of water," Betty agreed, fanning herself.

"Well, who is it?"

"If you'd been on time, I could have introduced you. But now I guess you'll just have to meet him on the way to the altar." Jenny waved to the wedding planner, who then cued the pianist to start playing.

Jenny turned on her heel and led us back out into the heat to await our groomsmen.

The groomsmen made their way out in matching t-shirts with 'Grooms Crew' on them. A snort sneaked out of me before I could stop it. John's brother, Tim, led the way. His best friend Adam and my cousin Junior followed behind. And then, to my eternal shock, I caught a glimpse of perfectly waved dark hair. It can't be him. I knew every other man in this town, and not a one had a head of hair worth writing home to mama about. He stepped to the side and I got my first full glimpse of Tucker Jones in that tight, black t-shirt. I felt my temperature climb five more degrees, and it wasn't because of the Georgia sun beating down on my bare shoulders.

Betty leaned in to whisper. "You lucky duck, she gave you the only eligible bachelor in this lineup. I've got to walk with Junior, and you've got the hot college friend. Life is just not fair." She openly gawked at him, and I had to squash a surge of jealousy. One tire change doesn't give me any right to be jealous.

About that time, Tucker looked over at me and I saw confusion cross his face for a brief moment, but before he had a chance to say anything, Jenny grabbed him by the arm and led him towards me. "Tucker Jones, this is my sister Marlie. Marlie, Tucker Jones. Y'all make nice now, ok? It's time to get this show on the road." With that whirlwind introduction over, she turned and sashayed to the back of the line.

The other pairs had already linked elbows for our practice walk down the aisle. Tucker gave me an affable grin, and stuck his elbow out in my direction. "So, Marleen, is it? Jenny really talked up her gorgeous read-headed sister, but I didn't dare dream it would be you."

I groaned. "She's the only one that calls me by my full name. I think at this point she just does it out of habit."

I wrapped my hand around his warm bicep, and it felt like my heart skipped a few beats being this close to him. Why did he have to be tall, handsome, kind, good at changing tires, and built like a god? Was somebody out there trying to kill me? I glared up at the heavens for the second time today, and nearly missed our cue to start down the aisle in the process.

Tucker led me through the doors of the sanctuary, and after the couple ahead of us made it about halfway down, the wedding planner waved us forward.

"So, I guess you really did have plans tonight, huh?" Tucker whispered. I whipped my head around to see if he was kidding but found his serene gaze locked ahead where John waited next to the pastor.

"Of course I had plans," I answered in a heated whisper, "Did you think I lied to you?"

I felt his shrug in response because the bicep where my happy hand was snuggled rose and fell as he did it.

"What kind of women do you usually ask out that they lie to avoid you?"

"Well, I tried to ask you out, but you turned me down. It is nice to know you weren't just blowing me off, though."

"Speaking of, you were asking me out to what, a rehearsal dinner? Isn't that an odd first date? Maybe that's why women turn you down." I muttered the last bit under my breath, not intending for him to hear it. We reached the front of the aisle and split off to our respective sides before he had a chance to answer.

Jenny jaunted down the aisle on our dad's arm to the pianist's enthusiastic bridal march, before being handed off to an eager John. The pastor said a few short words, and they sneaked a kiss before the planner sent us all out to do it over again. Tucker stuck his elbow back out for me to be escorted back out of the church, and I accepted it.

"I'll have you know, women don't usually turn me down," he said as we started down the aisle.

I laughed, "Ok, good for you, then."

"I just wouldn't want you to get the wrong impression, seeing as we'll be spending some time together over the course of the next few days," he drawled.

"Uh-huh," I responded noncommittally.

We reached the back door of the church, and he held it open for me to pass through, ever the gentleman. Once we were all lined back up outside, we started the whole shooting match over again.

"Should we be offended they don't seem to think we can all walk a straight line?" I asked no one in particular.

Betty snorted, "Some of us could use a little more practice than others." She gave Junior a pointed look, which he ignored.

"How many more times do we have to do this?" Tim asked the planner.

"One more time, and if y'all get it right we can head on over to supper. So don't screw it up." She said and pointed at him with a no-nonsense look in her eye. She then turned and signaled the pianist to start again as she made her way into the church.

With the first couples leading the way, we waited our turn huddled by the door.

"You know, if you want to talk about making assumptions—If I hadn't wanted to go out with you, I'd have just said so. I didn't need to lie about having plans." I said as we started our slow pace down the aisle.

The planner motioned exaggeratedly for me to pretend I was holding a bouquet, so I snapped my other arm into place. To my surprise, Tucker didn't say anything else for the rest of our trip down the aisle.

There you go again, Marlie. Always scaring off the handsome ones. I thought to myself and tuned out the pastor's pretend sermon. The planner motioned for us to make our exit again, so I met Tucker in front of the altar and took his elbow for our walk out.

About halfway down, he surprised me by asking, "So, does that mean you do, in fact, want to go out with me?"

"I'm sorry, how exactly did you come up with that idea?" My throat tightened, and I tried not to let my panic show through my voice.

"Let's call it a hunch that you would have said yes, if you didn't have this rehearsal dinner to attend." He looked over at me, grinning like the cat who just swallowed the canary.

I stayed silent, as I hadn't intended to give myself away like that. He's not wrong, if not for the embarrassing circumstances, I probably would have said yes. Maybe. What is wrong with me?

We exited the church yet again, and thankfully the planner was pleased with our two run-throughs and told us to head to the dinner portion of the evening. I let go of his arm and crossed mine across my chest instead. Before either one of us realized what was happening, Joanne swooped in and snagged his other arm.

"Why Tucker, do you think you could escort me over to the dinner? I'd love to hear about your latest business trip. What is it you do, exactly?" She batted her false eyelashes like a pro.

"Uh, well," Tucker looked over at me apologetically, "Sure, I can walk over with you. I think we'll all be walking together, though."

She laughed, and stroked his arm lightly, "Oh, Tucker, if I'm on your arm I don't think I'll notice what everyone else is doing."

Laying it on thick, Joanne. I rolled my eyes at her obvious flirtation and trailed towards the reception hall at the back of the boisterous group.

Dinner turned out to be spaghetti, and I mentally patted myself on the back for wearing black. I made a heaping plate and stacked a few slices of buttery garlic bread on the side for good measure. As I made my way back to the tables, I noticed that the only seat left was directly across from Tucker. The entire extended family made it over here before the wedding party, which wasn't too surprising given how much our family likes to eat.

I set my plate down carefully and managed not to knock any of the bread off onto the tablecloth. Right as I settled a napkin in my lap, Tucker abruptly stood from his seat.

"I'm going to go grab something to drink. You ladies want anything?" His voice came out even, but his eyes looked a little wild. "No? Ok, I'll be back." He hurried across the room to the drink table.

"Joanne, what are you doing to the poor man? He just about ran away from you. And scaring the men off is usually Marlie's job," Betty asked from her place next to me.

"I don't have the faintest idea what you're talking about," Joanne said innocently. "I just asked him if he had his eye on any of the desserts."

"Well, I'd give it up if I were you. He's clearly not interested in your sweets. You got that man running for cover," Betty said wryly.

Joanne sighed, "You're probably right, but you can't blame a girl for trying. I guess that means it's up to you, Marlie," she said, eyeing my mountain of spaghetti with her eyebrows raised in judgment.

"What are you talking about, up to me?" I asked, fork paused halfway to my mouth.

"We cannot let him out of this wedding without one of us attached to him. Look at that man! He needs a good southern girl in his life. And frankly, he is clearly looking to find someone if he came solo. He could have asked just about any available woman if he didn't want to come alone. Yet here he is, ripe for the picking." She waved her hand around the gathering as if this was all obvious.

My mind went back to the grocery store, where he'd asked a complete stranger to accompany him to this dinner, and I couldn't help but question her logic; it seemed to me he didn't want to be here alone.

"You better snap him up, Marlie!" Betty agreed and snapped her fingers in punctuation as Tucker returned to the table with a glass in hand.

"Did you ladies miss me?" Tucker asked with a smile as he sat back down, and his gaze lingered on me.

"You know it," Betty responded with a wink, but I just looked down at my spaghetti.

The next morning, the bride's room was engulfed in a veritable cloud of perfume and hairspray. Coughing, I tried to back out slowly, but Jenny spotted me and gestured in my direction, the stress plain on her face.

"Marlie! Thank God! I was worried you were going to be late again." She huffed out a breath towards her bangs, which having been curled and sprayed to within an inch of their lives, didn't budge.

I forced a smile, "No, definitely not. You are my number one focus today, Jenny. What can I help with?"

She worried her bottom lip between her teeth for a moment before answering, "Well, I need you to be honest with me. This is the most important day of my life. Do you think I picked the wrong eye shadow? I don't want it to clash with my lipstick."

My instinct was to chuckle at her dramatics, but her eyes were genuinely concerned, and I knew in that moment we'd gone past humor. "You look great, Jenny. When John sees you, he's going to be knocked off his boots with how beautiful you are." I gave her hands a squeeze, and she instantly relaxed.

"Oh Marlie, I love you, you know that? Once me and John are back from the honeymoon and settled, we're going to find someone for you to marry, too."

"Don't worry about me today, Jenny. Let's just get you down the aisle for now." I brushed off her promise of matchmaking. I hoped she'd forget all about it by the time she came home. A loud bang echoed in the room behind me, and I spun to see what caused the noise. Betty and Joanne had opened a bag of celebratory poppers. "Would you knock that off? Somebody's going to take a mascara wand to the eye!"

"Spoil sport!" Joanne said. "We're just keeping busy until it's our turn in the chair."

Betty elbowed her, and then zeroed in on me with a wicked gleam in her eye, "Why don't we talk about your plans with Tucker instead?"

Letting out a groan, I shook my head at her, "Can you two not let it rest? I am not the type to chase a man down; I prefer to let things happen of their own accord."

"How's that working out for you?" Joanne practically oozed sarcasm, "Sometimes you've got to get out there and push the envelope, girl. You are in the prime of your life, it's time to let loose a little."

A small part of me couldn't help but think that maybe she was right. The instant I spotted Tucker in the grocery store, I felt attraction spark between us. If it hadn't been for the peanut gallery roasting me on my age, maybe something would have happened of its own accord. But that ship had already sailed. Did that mean I had to write Tucker off, just because we met in a less-than-ideal way? He hadn't seemed overly put off last night at the rehearsal.

Betty chimed in before I had a chance to respond, "Word on the grape vine is that his ex-girlfriend will be attending the wedding tonight with her new man. I bet he snaps her back up in no time flat. That's what helped my Jackson along in getting back together with me, after all. One well-timed date and he was overcome with jealousy." She looked in my direction with pity before continuing, "Sorry, Marlie. But fine men like Tucker just don't hang around on the market forever."

"Y'all need to stop talking about that poor man like he's a piece of meat. And leave me out of it, too, would you?" I snapped, stung at the thought of Tucker with his ex.

"Marlie, I'm ready for you." The hairdresser gestured to her empty chair, and I hustled over to get away from Betty and Joann.

Nearly two hours later, we'd all been primped, prepped, and stuffed into bright purple bridesmaids gowns. The color didn't look too horrible, even though I'd have never picked it for myself. I attempted to pat the large fabric flower down away from my face, but it sprang right back up like a perky nightmare for the thousandth time since I'd donned the dress.

The wedding planner arrived at the bride's room door and announced that it was time to start the ceremony. Butterflies took flight in my stomach at the thought of seeing Tucker in a moment, and I tried to shove the feeling down. I wasn't the one getting hitched today, so I had nothing to be nervous about. Except falling flat on my face in these shoes. I glanced down at the offending peep-toed purple footwear. They may have been ankle death traps, but they showed off my freshly painted nails to perfection.

I fell into step behind Jenny, holding up the end of her voluminous train as we made our way through the very full parking lot to wait outside the sanctuary door. The gaggle of suited groomsmen gathered there jostled each other, but quieted as we approached, and then separated to find their assigned bridesmaids. The fifteen pounds of pure white satin had my arms burning, and I gratefully sat it down.

Tucker whistled slowly as he approached and took me in, "Why Marlie, you are a vision in purple."

"Stop it. This is not my color!" The blush took over my face with a vengeance, the curse of redheads everywhere.

He proffered his elbow genially, "Beauty is in the eye of the beholder, and I think you'd be gorgeous in a potato sack. So, I guess you'll just have to get used to it," he said and gave me a sly wink.

My hand clutched his jacket sleeve tightly at his words, and I forced it to relax. I looked at him sideways and took in the full picture that is Tucker Jones in a tux. The sight of him was enough to buckle my knees; he's got "tall, dark, and handsome" on lock, and his hair had just the slightest wave to it where he'd styled it back for the occasion. His warm chocolate brown eyes drew me in the minute I saw them. Although, my favorite thing about him so far was that no matter what, he was always smiling.

The door to the church opened, and we could hear the pianist playing as the first pair headed for the aisle. We all slowly made our way forward, and the snail-like pace of the procession gave me plenty of time to feel the warmth radiating off of Tucker. When it was our turn, we paced sedately down the aisle. My eyes flitted over the gathered crowd before coming to an abrupt stop on a curvy blonde in a tight green gown. Her acidic glare stood out in stark contrast to the crowd of well-wishers.

I whispered discretely to Tucker while trying to keep my smile fixed in place, "Do you know that woman? She is glaring at us fit to set us on fire."

He tensed, as he followed my gaze and spotted the woman in question, "Unfortunately I do," was all he had time to say before we arrived at the flower-be-decked altar and had to go our separate ways.

The ceremony passed in a beautiful blur. Jenny and John beamed at each other with all the hope of a new life together. I tried my best not to, but I still teared up a little as they said their vows so sweetly. My tears turned to laughter when after the pastor announced them, John tossed Jenny over his shoulder and carried her down the aisle.

The rest of us quickly made our way out for photos, and then on to the reception.

My mood was light as Tucker held the door for me, and then led me over to the drink selection. He quickly procured two sweet teas for us, and then we turned to take in the happy crowd. "Jenny and John sure are good together, don't you think?"

"I do, they seem really happy together. I'm glad for them," I responded. Across the room, the angry blonde spotted us and headed our way.

"Marlie, I need your help with something."

"Sure, what's up?"

"Just don't slap me, okay?"

"What?" I looked over at him in confusion. Why in the world would I slap him?

Before I could ask, the blonde broke through the crowd with a tall man in tow, and Tucker turned to me, slid both hands around my waist, and planted a kiss directly on my lips. My brain short-circuited, and the warmth of his kiss felt like it rolled over my entire body in an instant. My hands drifted up to the back of his neck seemingly of their own accord, and the rest of me melted into his hard chest.

After a small eternity, he pulled back and took in my glazed expression.

"What was that for?" My hand went to my lips. I was both excited and confused by this turn of events.

"Really, Tucker? Way to be mature about this!" The angry blonde stormed off, dragging the hapless man in her wake.

My mouth dropped open. "Who was that, exactly?"

For the first time, Tucker looked abashed, "My ex. Susan. I'm sorry for the impromptu kiss, but she's been hounding me for nearly a month. She cheated on me with her co-worker."

"Oh," I responded. "Happy to be of service, then." Deflated, I sat my tea glass down and beat a hasty retreat to the hallway. I had nearly made it to the ladies' room when a masculine hand snagged my wrist, stopping me mid-flight.

"Marlie, please wait! I wanted to kiss you." His voice was strained.

I spun angrily, "Really Tucker, did you? Or was it just a show for your ex?" I said the last bit quietly, hoping to avoid fueling the gossip that I was sure had already started to spread like wildfire through the reception.

"No, Marlie, I wanted to kiss you. I've wanted to kiss you since yesterday when I asked you out the first time." His eyes pleaded with mine for understanding, and he slipped his hand down from my wrist to hold my hand.

"Why me, Tucker? You could have your pick of women in this room. Including your ex, who's over there glaring at your back as we speak," I stated, finally letting my insecurity peek through.

He raked a hand through his perfectly styled hair in agitation, "I'm not interested in giving her another minute of my time, Marlie. I can promise you that." He stilled, and then ever so slowly reached a hand up to brush an escaped strand of hair back behind my ear. "Because, the minute I saw you in that grocery store, I was hooked. You were so kind to Mrs. Lindy, even when she embarrassed you. You kept your head high, and you had this look on your face, like . . . I don't even know," he paused, seeming to run it through in his mind, "You looked like you were going to charge a hungry bear with nothing but a biscuit."

A startled laugh escaped me at his absurd comparison, and he smiled softly in return, running his thumb over my chin.

"I knew in that moment that you were used to taking it on the chin, and making the best of things. You aren't the kind of person that lets life get you down, no matter the hand you're dealt. You're stronger than you give yourself credit for, Marlie. And I'd like the chance to get to know you better. So, it seems I'll have to ask you again, would you please go on a date with me? Because I need a repeat of that kiss."

Could I let myself take a chance with him—really go all in? I took in his earnest expression, and in that moment, I decided to trust him. Sometimes, you have to go out on a limb to get what you want.

"Tucker Jones, I'd like to go on a date with you." I stated matter-of-factly.

His expression morphed into a wide grin at my bold proclamation, "Marlie Abernathy, I'd like to go on a date with you. How does tomorrow night sound?"

"It sounds perfect."

Epilogue – One Year Later

Betty and Jackson's wedding was a lovely evening. The outdoor ceremony was quaint and festive, with friends and family all around. I glanced over at Tucker as he sipped his sweet tea and chatted with John like the old friends they were. Jenny rubbed her baby bump as she leaned on John's arm contentedly. It'd been nice to have a handsome man to call my own tonight.

The last year, really. Tucker and I had taken that first date, and then another, and another. Before long we were so wrapped up in each other that we decided after six months we'd rather not keep living in different towns. So, Tucker packed up and rented the little house right next door to his Great-aunt Celia, only ten minutes from me. Turns out, life's just better with your other half, no matter when or how you find them. His smile still makes me weak-kneed, just like it did on that first day.

The DJ interrupted my musings, "If I could get all of the single ladies to the dance floor for the bouquet toss, Betty is ready to give it away to one lucky lady!"

I snorted, watching several teenagers elbowing each other for prime positions. Jenny grabbed my arm, "You better get out there!"

"Jenny, I don't know if you know this or not, but I'm happily no longer single. Haven't been single a day in the last year," I protested.

"Until there is a ring on that finger, you are still single. Now get!" She shoved my shoulders. I rolled my eyes at Tucker, but rather than argue with my pregnant sister I made my way to the dance floor.

Betty made a big show of the countdown, but when it was time to toss the bouquet over her shoulder, she spun around and put it straight into my waiting hands.

"Betty! What are you doing? You're supposed to toss it!" I laughed at her antics. When I turned around to show Jenny, I froze in my tracks. Because there, settled in the middle of the dance floor on one knee with a diamond ring in his hand, was Tucker Jones.

"Tucker, what are you doing?" My voice shook with the question.

"Well, you see, I thought it was high time we made this official. So, I wanted to ask you, Marlie, if you'd do me the honor of becoming my wife," he said, and to my utter surprise, I picked up a hint of tension in his jawline.

"Tucker Jones, there is nothing that would make me happier than to be your wife," I said softly.

He surged to his feet, and in one smooth motion drew me into a blistering kiss. His arms held me tight to his chest, and he gently rested his forehead against mine, his grin ear-to-ear. I threaded a hand into his thick hair and grinned back. He wants me, forever.

"It's about time you locked him down, sugar! You ain't getting any younger!" The shout from the crowd startled me, and we broke apart to see old Mrs. Lindy cheering us on.

At that, we both busted out laughing. Some things will never change. But sometimes, life can surprise you in the best possible ways. I looked into Tucker's shining eyes and I couldn't wait to see what surprises life had in store for us.

Before You Go . . .

Thank you so much for reading Bea Mine! I do hope you enjoyed it (and the bonus short story!), and are looking forward to the next book in the series as much as I enjoyed writing it. As a new author, your review means the world to me. If you would take a moment to leave a rating or review before you go on to your next read, I would be over the moon to see it.

If you'd like to sign up for my mailing list so you never miss a new release, and get fun freebies from time to time like recipes, short stories, and more, you can do so here (subscribepage.com/KristenDi xon)!

I am available by email at kristendixonauthor@gmail.com as well, if you'd ever like to drop me a line directly!

Also By Kristen Dixon

Bless Your Heart (FREE!!!!!)
Thirty and unmarried in the south, can Marlie find
her forever wedding date? A romantic short story
sure to make you smile.

Bea Mine (Sweet Nothings Bake Shop, Book 1)
**The quirky baker. Her best friend's off-limits older
brother. When sparks—and frosting—fly between
them, it'll be a Valentine's Day to remember.**
When two stubborn southerners don't see eye to
eye, it's bound to cause sparks. But if these two can't

see heart to heart, it might just be the worst mistake the small town of Adele, Georgia has ever seen. This clean contemporary novella will have you falling in love from the first chapter.

Will Travel for Love (Sweet Nothings Bake Shop, Book 2)

A small town girl. An alluring British engineer who's just passing through. Will she follow her head, or lose her heart?

Check out book two of the Sweet Nothings Bake Shop series, and see what Celia's got up her sleeve for Daphne. Or should we say, who she's got up her sleeve?

Waiting on Forever (Sweet Nothings Bake Shop, Book 3)

She's healing from the blindside of divorce. He's a small-town hero. Can they build something together, or will it all fall apart?

With the two of them at odds, tension builds in the most unlikely of ways. Will her stubborn pride keep her lonely forever, or will Jensen be able to prove he's got enough heart to share with Maggie and her daughter?

The Bachelor Bargain (Sweet Nothings Bake Shop, Book 4)
An outspoken graphic designer. The town's most introverted bachelor. Will they open up to each other, or will the town's zany attempts at match-making push them further apart?
One sunset dinner won't change a thing . . . until it changes *everything*.

The Ferguson Brothers Series (coming 2023)

About the Author

Kristen Dixon was born and raised in Jacksonville, Florida, and is happily married with two kids. She has worked as a restaurant hostess, library book shelver, ranch hand, trail riding guide, and about twelve other unrelated fields, because variety—and sweet tea—is the spice of life. Not to mention a little thing called pursuing her passion of writing. She likes to write late in the evenings and thinks baking great cookies fuels hopes and dreams.

Her books are sweet, clean, and southern with real heart. If you like a classic southern gentleman, quirky side characters, and small towns, well, y'all came to the right place. Grab some tea, pull up a chair, and get ready to sit a spell.

If you would like to get all the latest news about her works, you can sign up for her newsletter at h ttps://www.subscribepage.com/KristenDixon and as always, don't forget to Follow on Amazon!